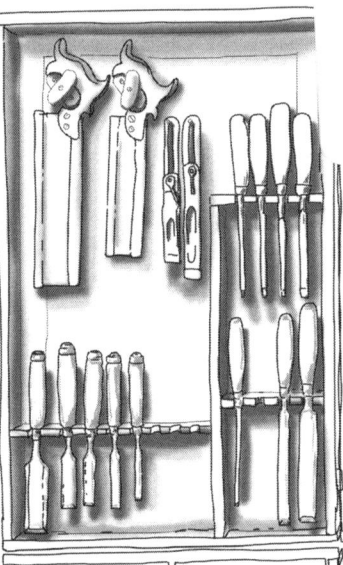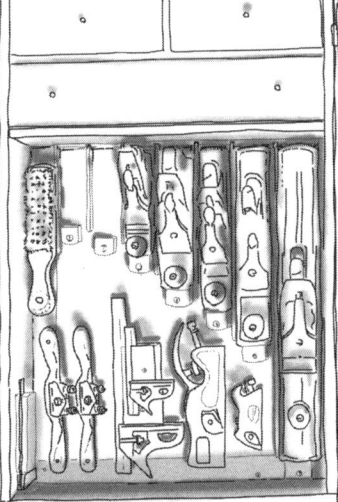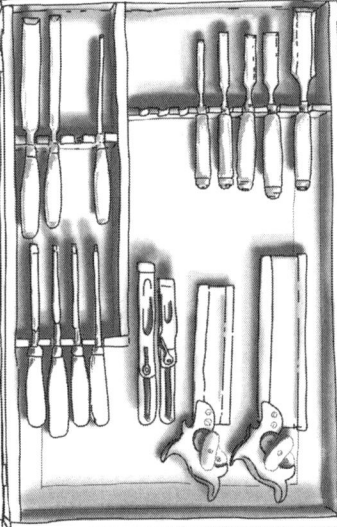

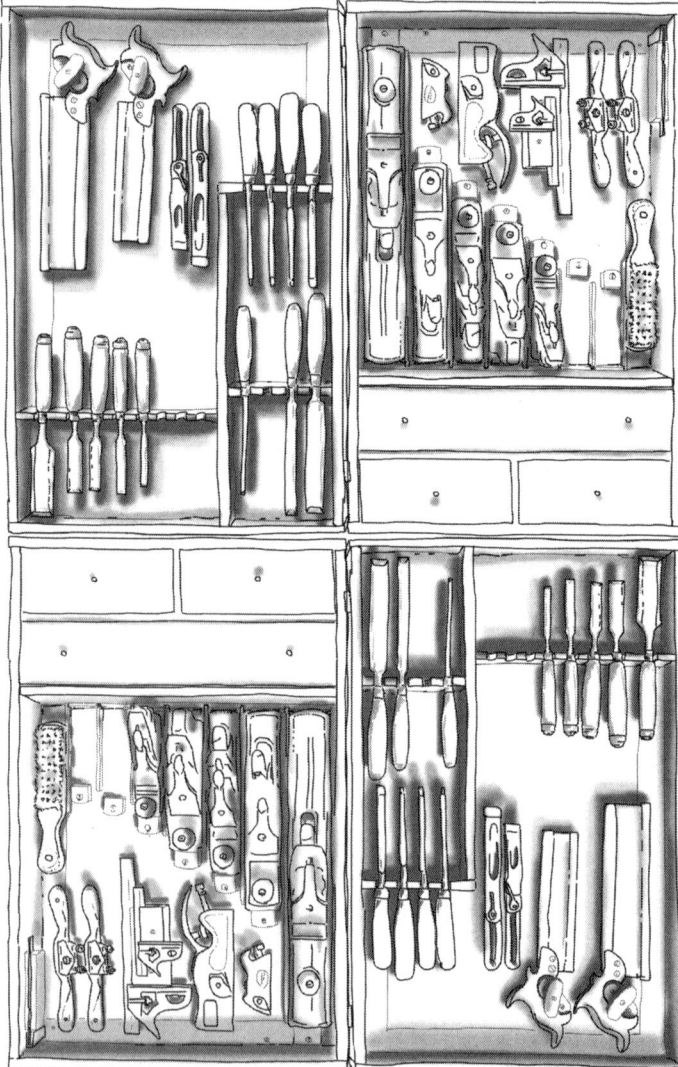

THE JOSEPHS
AND OTHER STORIES

Polly Tuckett

First published in 2020
by Stonewood Press
Diversity House
72 Nottingham Road, Arnold
Nottingham NG5 6LF
books@stonewoodpress.co.uk
www.stonewoodpress.co.uk

All rights reserved
Copyright © Polly Tuckett, 2020
The author asserts her moral right to be
indentified as the author of this work

ISBN: 978-1-910413-31-9 (paperback)
ISBN: 978-1-910413-32-6 (ebook)

Represented by Inpress, tel: 0191 230 8104
enquiries@inpressbooks.co.uk
Distributed by NBN International

Printed & bound in the UK by Imprintdigital, Exeter

Designed and typeset in Minion 10.5pt/12.5pt
by www.silbercow.co.uk
Cover illustration and endpapers by Martin Parker

Acknowledgement:
For their help and inspiration, thanks to my family,
(especially Oscar & Rita), Jacqueline Gabbitas,
Martin Parker, Geoffrey Bennington, Véronique
Voruz and all my well-wishing friends – PT

This is the eighth book in the THUMBPRINT series

Contents

The Terrible Mountains 5

The Josephs 19

The Cat With No Name 31

The Terrible Mountains

ou had to trust that your survival instinct would kick in, trust the will to control the body and determine a positive outcome. How could she know that whether on purpose or due to inexperience she wouldn't veer off to the left into that stand of fir trees?

The white expanse was like death itself. Her weakness was a drug coursing through her body, taking hold. Her legs were trembling and her feet inside the unyielding boots felt as though they were swimming in blood. The only way was down, although she could take sidewise penguin steps up the mountain to the ski lift. But no, she couldn't – look at those empty chairs sailing free on their way back. Paolo was dead. And she had to get down the mountain; she, an alien, placing her faith in the manmade prosthetics jutting from her feet. Sick of the drama, the tumultuous poeticisms and pseudo-philosophical pronouncements clamouring in her mind, she could not, though, distance herself from them.

The skis were pointed downwards, ready for the plunge. All around her people seemed glibly cheerful – determined, achieving, capable – people who knew not to question the sense of all things. A three year-old whooshed past, slaloming stylishly down the slope. The lift was passing overhead, the people sitting on the stupid little chairs seemingly unconcerned, legs dangling high above the abyss. And the sky so relentlessly blue. A set of feelings gripped her, nameless, overwhelming, and ice in her stomach.

Earlier that day she'd been taught snow plough on the nursery slopes, but now her knees wouldn't bend right and the valley was rushing up towards her. She leaned back, lost a stick and swerved to avoid someone. Her skis crossed and ejected her. The jolt to her tailbone as she hit the ground brought tears to her eyes and once she started crying she couldn't stop. Something more than physical incapacity, a deep humiliation in relying on the body to do what it should and finding that it would not. She couldn't cry about Paolo, even though she spent her whole time thinking about him, yet here she was blubbing like a baby because she'd hurt herself.

There had been warning signs right from the start. But weren't there always? He told her about a story he was writing in which a woman asked her lover to murder her. When they started sleeping together he put his hands around her throat and started choking her, reminding her of a group exercise in a Theatre Studies class where you had to fall backwards, trusting you'd be caught. She told him she wasn't into it and he never did it again.

She spat out snow and brushed it off her face and the plastic bib of her neon salopettes, sitting up. A woman with white lipstick and reflective goggles swished to a neat stop beside her and asked in German if she was OK.

'Yes,' she answered in English.

'Is this your stick?'

'Yes, thanks.'

The woman helped her to her feet.

'Will you be all right?'

'Yes,' she said. The woman skied off. Edith picked up her skis and trudged down the mountain to the next station. When she got there her mum, dad and brothers were waiting for her.

'Have you been crying?'

'No,' she said.

After a while her dad and brothers took off and Edith sat with her mum on the veranda drinking Schnapps. She felt heat flood to her face. The snow was dazzling and the people were insects crawling about on it. Exposed rock on the mountains opposite appeared harsh, like wounds.

'This is too much for you, isn't it? We don't have to do any more skiing if you don't want to. You can get the lift down from here.'

The next day they went skating because she hated skiing so much. The lake was covered with a fine mantle of snow and scarred with the tracks of ice skates and paw prints. Shelf ice massed at the edges and the long spikes of candle ice pitted the surface nearer the middle, which was bluish white from impurities in the water. The ice was at least a foot thick but it creaked and groaned alarmingly as it split into rifts, great jagged continents forming beneath Edith's feet.

A young girl whirled past, twizzling and flinging her arms about like a ballerina. The bloom on her cheeks and the soft hat, pinks and whites, her dewy youth and delicate eyelashes, the simple joy – Edith felt a stab of envy, wishing she could exchange her life. Her mum held her hand tightly as they skated tentatively out towards the far end of the lake. There was no need for words. Everything was dwarfed by the terrible mountains.

One night, unable sleep, she grabbed her diary. I would rather, she wrote, that he died than that he left me. When he'd been gone without news for so long, already dead, she had dreamed up fantasies of deception, him with another woman, laughing at her, or worse, oblivious to her. And then she found out that the night she wrote her diary was the night he died. Did this make her a witch?

The holiday was a mad idea and she'd been shoehorned into it. They were there with her brothers' public school and she found the noise and the exaggerated Englishness of the party unbearable. So the ice skating was an escape. Her mum was wearing the black velvet coat with the real fur collar she'd had since the 70s. In the bright light its worn patches took on a gunmetal sheen. They lurched and stumbled as they went round the lake, keeping each other up.

Was she unlovable? Her mum loved her – well, she had to. He had claimed to love her too but it was a fad, his love for her, it hadn't lasted. It was all poses, brilliant facets. She needed to be loved more than she could offer love. In feeling adored she was at her most loving, most expansive. When she tried to isolate characteristics that would make her lovable to someone else she was at a loss. But then she had always suspected that she didn't really have a personality. She was just a being, filtering experience through a consciousness that had been shaped in this way or that to interpret the world. But this was avoidance. Thinking about his failed love for her in no way mitigated the impact of the loss of him. Remembering his bad temper in the mornings, his refusal to ever wash his work trousers, his love of avocados and Reese's Peanut Butter Cups, his dry sense of humour, she was reminded that these were just examples of who she understood him to be, outer manifestations or accidents of fortune, preferences and modes of expression, not him in any essential way – their specificity seemingly revealing a uniqueness and irreplaceability which was really only 'original' in its one-off constellation of repeatable particularities – and so, like her, there was no essential him – he was a hollow soul, a flame of being, and they had been twin flames for a time.

As Edith and her mum walked back from the lake the evening sun stained the snows crimson. Deciduous trees with their dark bark were silhouetted like lungs against the sky, lacy forms, indecipherable as symbols in a dream. Beauty hurt her; perceiving it, she experienced vicious little stabs of sorrow and self-pitying bitterness.

Back at the hostel, the kids were making a racket and the adults were being grotesquely jovial around the trestle tables. She couldn't manage a single mouthful and excused herself as soon as she could to wander the streets of the little town. A huge Christmas tree stood on an island in the middle of the street. Presents hung from the branches and Edith smiled, remembering her disappointment as a child on discovering these were fake when she stole one from the school tree and opened it in the toilets. Stuffing the empty cardboard box and wrapping paper into the bin, she had covered her crime with paper towels.

It was snowing, little polka dots on the night. Someone once told her there was no such thing as bad weather, only inadequate clothing. She shivered pulling her collar up. The cobbled streets were narrow and the shop fronts mesmerising, their goods displayed with tantalizing negligence. A watch shop had a Christmassy diorama with a toy train driven by a waistcoated rabbit, the wagons filled with tiny clock parts and exorbitantly priced watches draped here and there over the glittering fibreglass snow banked high around the tracks, as if you could just reach in and pluck one out.

She looked up and noticed a man walking away from her down the street. From the back he looked just like Paolo. Yes, he was walking exactly like him, purposefully and with a slight stoop. The coat could be his, the hair, everything. It could be him! This whole nightmare might be some sick joke, God or Disney's way of teaching her a lesson. Perhaps he was not really leaving her. Maybe his death was a malicious rumour. She followed him, her brisk walk breaking into a jog. Her ribcage constricted like a claw; she could hardly breathe. He turned down a side street. Now he was entering a café bar. She followed him in, wanting and not wanting to get a good look at him. He went to the toilets in the back. She ordered a liqueur coffee. But when he came out his face was all wrong. She took her coffee to a table in the corner and sat facing the window with her back to the clientele. She was so stupid. Furious, her shoulders shook and tears ran down her cheeks. The impostor left the café and passed in front of the window. Now, not even his gait seemed familiar as he ambled off down the street. She'd been tricked, life had played on her another vile trick.

She took out a compact mirror and dabbed at her eyes with a manky old tissue. She paid and walked, dazed, out into the street. All the shops were so expensive, so cruel and smug a contrast, all the wealth in such harsh conditions. What if you were homeless? – and what was the answer to that? – aren't we the lucky ones? She looked at a pair of leather boots in one window, at a deep-pile rug in another and then stopped, spellbound, in front of a jeweller's window. There was an exquisite ring, a diamond solitaire. It didn't have a price tag.

A bell rang as Edith entered the shop. She asked to see the ring and as the shopkeeper went to fetch it from the window she felt slightly giddy and found herself clutching the glass counter. To go into debt would be a kind of relief, it would give her something else to worry about, something more tangible. She took off her glove and tried the ring on her wedding finger. It was a perfect fit. She asked the price. It was a staggering sum and would take her to the limit of her overdraft. She paid by cheque.

There was a woman who married herself, maybe a friend of a friend, or else an urban myth. It seemed stupid to her, exhibitionist, futile. Edith was alone too, but engaged to a ghost, the man who left her first then died, as if to make his point. No one else would bear witness. She could pretend though, a fake wedding with a real ring. The snow was falling fast. She held up her hand. The diamond winked, complicit with the snowflakes. She remembered him coming up behind her, wrapping his arms around her waist and kissing her neck. 'Cutchin my love, I'll never leave you.' 'Cutchin' was the name of his cat, he couldn't even be bothered to invent a personal nickname for her.

The dizziness would pass. She hadn't eaten all day. Her skin felt tight on her face. She was young, the cold reminded her of this fact, usually something to revel in but now she experienced a sense of bitter pointlessness. Life stretched ahead, a too-bright tunnel. She would never again find love like this, a forcefield around her chest. That she could carry on, put one foot in front of the other, seemed impossible, sickmaking.

She returned to the hostel. She borrowed a floaty white nightie from her mum, put it on and sat writing at the cramped little desk.

Antidepressants. Well they definitely weren't cutting it now. He used to go on at her about them, accusing her of being weak and polluting herself, talking about silenced lawsuits against Big Pharma and calcification of the pineal gland and a million other side effects. She couldn't remember the exact phrases, only the substance of his rants. Often there was some kind of truth at the heart of what he was saying but he would exaggerate, blame all the usual scapegoats. He subscribed to various crackpot conspiracy theories. His relationship to others was aristocratic and he included her in this self-aggrandizing exclusivity, sealing them off in a pod from the rest of humanity. He believed in originality. Other women were 'poobots' he claimed, dismissing anyone well groomed or self-possessed. She did not appear polished to him – he thought she had no grace. She picked her nose in front of him and he called her a scruff. He too was a graceless scruff and used to piss into milk bottles. But the same things she was accusing him of, she too was guilty of. Hadn't she judged all the other skiiers in the same way the day before, and made of herself the only feeling subject?

She wrote about this and about the torture of a love that couldn't be returned. Love was a gift, unfreely given, it demanded payment in kind. She wrote furiously, scribbled down her thoughts as fast as they came. She begged God to return him to her, promising to convert. She described his eyes as stars and didn't care if it sounded clichéd. In the past she would write her diary fully expecting him to read it. She couldn't shake the feeling he was still reading.

That night she didn't really sleep but entered a dream state where it seemed certain that he was watching over her and that everything would be all right. She became aware of his presence as a dark angel with massive coppery wings. He stooped at her shoulder and whispered in her ear, but she couldn't catch what he was saying.

When she woke from this semi-dream, a crick in her neck and her head on the desk, she resolved to join him in the hereafter, if there was to be one, and if not then in nothingness. She stood up and got dressed. It was still dark outside. The lights were on in the hall and the receptionist buzzed her out. The street was deserted. She walked quickly through the town. She strode out across the snowy plains. The faintest tinge of blue and gold gilded the mountaintops. The snow reflected this light. Then the sun came up and with it searing shades of persimmon and damask rose blooming in the sky. Again, she rejected the beauty which moved her and kept her eyes to the ground. She was walking through woods now, still in the valley but on an incline.

This was a cowardly way out. Not suicide itself but the means of doing it, exposure. Like someone swimming out to sea letting nature do her dirty work. She kept walking on and on. She was climbing now and had left the kitsch chalets far behind. The whiteness of the snow hurt her eyes. Why couldn't it be black, shimmering like jet beads, absorbing its own sparkle? She felt for the diazepam in her pocket. Six left, ten milligrams. She swallowed them one by one, melting snow in her mouth. She was sweating inside the bubble jacket so she took it off and carried it. Minutes passed and she began to feel woozy. She lay her coat on the snow and curled up on it. The sensation of a rubber mallet to the cerebellum and the shutters came down.

A friendly face in hers, inhuman. Wetness on her nose, across her cheeks. Furry face smiling, mouth open, slavering. A silver blanket. And now being held, jolted, carried across the uneven ground despite her extreme mass. Like mercury, she could plummet down through a stomach's wall.

When Edith woke up she was inside a cabin, swaddled in blankets in front of a fire. She stared into the flames feeling the luxury of heat on her face. She could hear competing radio stations, voices and jingles. The telly was on, and another telly too, no three tellys showing CNN, a Russian news channel, a Chinese channel and in the corner, a laptop showing Al Jazeera. All over the walls were newspaper cuttings, maybe for insulation. She became aware of a throbbing pain in her fingers and toes. She closed her eyes.

The door opened. She looked up. A man approached with mugs of something. He crouched down beside her.

'Drink this,' he said.

She took a sip of the drink.

'What is it?' she asked him, her voice slurred.

'It's mulled wine,' he said, 'my only concession to Christmas.'

'It's nice,' said Edith.

'You're lucky I found you. You can't have been there long.'

She said nothing and took another sip of the hot wine. Right then a wolf padded into the room, its fur smoky dark and its eyes uncannily blue. It came up to her and licked her face, its black lips like a bicycle's inner tube. She stroked back the soft bristles on its head. Her stomach rumbled.

'You're hungry,' said the man. He went to the kitchen and she carried on fussing the dog.

'My saviour,' she whispered. When the man came back it was with a plate of buttered toast. She ate all three bits.

'Do you want some more?' he asked her.

'No, it's ok,' she said, although she could have eaten the whole loaf.

She asked him what was with all the news stories. He told her that he had to piece together some kind of truth about what was going on globally.

'But you're so isolated here, so far removed from the world.'

'Yes and no.'

'So how can you filter out the bias of each particular news source?'

'You can't. But one so often contradicts the other that it gives you a sense of what's at stake. Some are more balanced than others in their outlook, but I change channels all the time.'

'Yes, but when you have a media mogul controlling most of the news you can't take the median approach.'

'I'm not a statistician. I have my own filter and ways of seeking truth. And I read alternative news websites too. I form opinions only to reject them. I think I get the general gist.'

'But what's the point if you're not going to change the world?'

He smiled at her and didn't answer. Slowly she got to her feet. He said he would walk with her and show her the way back to the town. It was a long walk and she'd better get going before night fell.

They walked in silence down through the firs, which shed huge clumps of snow from time to time. She threw sticks for the dog, who never seemed to tire of the game. At the edge of the woods the man pointed the way to her and said goodbye.

'Here, take this diamond ring,' she said, 'you can buy some more tellys.'

The man laughed, accepted the ring and she set off. She felt lighter, almost joyous. The virgin snows lay as icing sugar on the ground in soft pleats and folds. On the topmost layer were impressions of bird feet, like little twigs.

The Josephs

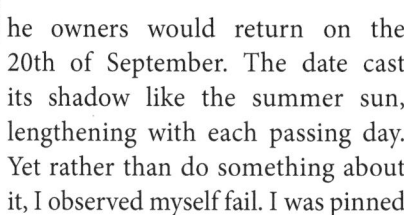

he owners would return on the 20th of September. The date cast its shadow like the summer sun, lengthening with each passing day. Yet rather than do something about it, I observed myself fail. I was pinned to the spot with a mix of dread, inertia and a kind of grim curiosity. It seemed to me that I had entered a world of abstraction, but the consequences of my lack of action would be all too real. I imagined the showdown with the family, their frustration and disappointment, my own ruined reputation, and felt criminal.

Pretending I was just a passer-by, I liked to observe the house from the opposite side of the street. Partially obscured by its tattoo of orange ivy, the patchy render on the outer walls complemented the leprous trunks of the plane trees that erupted from the tarmac at intervals along the pavement. Eleven stone steps led up to the front door.

Passing between the formal columns propping the doorway's crumbling lintel made me feel blessed but somehow doomed, like the character in a tragic tale. Nature always overtakes design in the end; nature becomes the design, or else the design reverts to nature.

Indoors too, was a pageant of decline. I wanted to leave the exposed plaster work as it was – for as long as I could get away with it, in any case. The walls were a tableau of gorgeous flaking mocha pinks and golds, shades of sienna and burnt umber, earth and clay. Artists work so hard to achieve this same palette that had been randomly thrown up by the renovation project, suggesting to me that process, as ever, is more valuable than the end result.

All this mellowing and ageing, this golden dilapidation, was somehow comforting to a man who suspected he might be in the throes of an inverted sort of midlife crisis – inverted because I wasn't so much fighting the grimness of a future that must stop with death, as flinging myself headlong into it. I think I was becoming obsessed with the idea of decay; that moment which is both the height of a thing's beauty and the signal of its decline. Before it wilts, a rose exposes itself most fully, its scent cloyingly sweet but with a bitter note like muscovado sugar.

Francesca, my lover, had left me. This was a relief. It meant I could become myself more fully.

I dropped my keys onto the kitchen table, scattered with crumbs from last night's meal, fetched a sponge and wiped it down, the water beading irritatingly on the oilskin tablecloth. At the counter I sliced bread onto a plate, cutting my finger and mopping up the blood with a paper serviette. I fetched marmalade from the cupboard. Scraping my knife around inside the jar, I had to concede it was empty. Then, ridiculously, I started crying. There was an orange grove at the foot of the hill, but for some insane reason I had it sent from England, dismissing the thought of the air miles. Pretty early on into my stay here, the guilt that had pervaded my entire existence drove me into the local church.

In Catholicism I hoped to find a rationale for this guilt, and perhaps to expiate a part of it too at confession, which was free, unlike the years of psychoanalysis in London. When I found the church to be empty, sheer nosiness drove me on. I knocked and, without expecting an answer, tried the door-handle.

The sacristy was brown and gold. A mighty sunbeam lit a portion of the room. It was a jumble sale in there, high-ceilinged and cluttered with packing cases, bicycle parts, candlesticks. On the counter I noticed a kettle and an open packet of noodles. Draped over a stack of boxes was a lushly embroidered robe. There was a crumpling sound and as my eyes adjusted to the gloom beyond the god-beam, I discerned the newspaper and the pair of reading glasses glinting over its shallow V. I'd disturbed his solitary breakfast. The priest folded his paper. 'I'm Father Ignatio,' he said, polishing off his pastry, 'and you're that builder fellow, aren't you?'

'Algernon. Algernon Renfrew'.

In bleak, world-hating moments, I blamed the person I'd become on my given name. Since playground days, I'd fled this identity. Algae, they'd taunted, pondweed. But in a foreign land even a silly name could take on a certain dignity. Ignatio in any case was hardly better.

'How can I help?' asked Father Ignatio.

'I want to convert.' I blurted it out.

The priest stared at me before a wry, disbelieving smile crept over his face.

'You'll forgive me,' he said, 'but in our faith, people don't often show up on the doorstep like this. We don't go out converting either. Just like you wouldn't really expect a Rabbi to go door-to-door spreading the word... Jehovah's Witnesses, yes, but the older religions don't need to work so hard.'

'Are you saying it's a closed shop? Members only?'

'No,' said Father Ignatio, standing to brush the crumbs from his cassock, 'no, of course not. So what, may I ask, has brought you here?'

He was a lovely laconic fellow, handsome too. I found myself confiding in him, trying to impress him with my candour. We ate dinner together that night and got through a couple of bottles of wine. His place was ornate, not at all what I would have expected. We sat in throne-like inlaid chairs at opposite ends of the table. He had this little poodle that kept jumping up, begging for scraps which he bestowed with an indulgent giggle. We agreed that I would not have to study the catechism but could jump straight to baptism and confirmation in one go, but first he would help find me a sponsor.

In the meantime, I had to get on with the house. I'd agreed to effect the major renovations, then the plastering and paintwork, and finally to begin work on a set of bespoke furniture. At first, I'd thrown myself into the structural work, humming as I wheeled rubble down a planked ramp, imagining the neighbours admiring my industriousness. And the work provided a good enough reason for avoiding Francesca. But once she'd gone, I took a breather from the renovation project and busied myself temporarily with the furniture instead. For two whole months now, I'd been working on a set of chairs, whittling their facings with a cranky perfectionism that somehow would not release me for the much more pressing task of finishing the house.

Not doing the house probably used up more mental energy than actually getting down to it. Some nights I woke sweating, resolving to work from dawn till nightfall and have the downstairs finished inside of a week. But when morning came, there were always reasons not to.

My sponsor was an old lady from the town. She asked me to choose a saint. The first to pop into my head was Mary Magdalene.

The more I grew to like Ignatio, the more the act of confession became an exercise in hypocrisy, with each peccadillo milder and more sweetly endearing than the last: 'Father I have sinned… I was guilty of covetousness when gazing at the F430 coupé Ferrari in a car magazine…'

My sins were so everyday, so lacking in the spirit of true perversity, that by contrast my seeming honesty in owning up to them ought to have flagged up my innate goodness, except that Ignatio was clever and saw through it.

'Come now,' he'd coax, 'I'm sure you can do better than that.'

Becoming a Catholic made me feel both glamorous and normal. The more senior villagers (the younger ones rarely attended mass) now greeted me familiarly in the street.

Francesca had worked out my new spiritual position once our sex life, never that great to begin with, began to tail off.

'The Pope's hands are stained with blood. Across the world millions are dying and all because a celibate man dictates that contraception is a sin!'

She was right, but did she have to be so strident? When I asked her to keep her voice down, she accused me of being a bourgeois curtain twitcher. But I thought it somehow far more bourgeois not to care what the neighbours thought.

'Well?' she asked.

'I take the doctrine with a pinch of salt. It's the ritual I'm interested in.'

But the opposite was true – it was rules that I craved, not ceremony.

I had no ambition, according to Francesca. No drive. She packed her things.

The house was too large. I lived within two of its rooms. I rarely used my voice inside. The mocking echo creeped me out. I liked to think of myself as a free spirit, craving only space and light, but the solitude was much harder than I'd anticipated. I suspect that like most people, my true desire was to hunker down for winter, to eat and sleep, to love and be loved, but I did not know how to go about realising this simple dream.

The truth was I hadn't loved Francesca. We had never really known one another. I found her enthusiasm grating, and once withdrawn, briefly heartbreaking, restoring to my perception of her the essential mystery that I supposed to be a part of woman's nature, rather than just my failure to imagine what it must be like to be a woman. This mystery had something to do with unattainability. Whereas women appeared to seek the meeting point between the sexes, men were more interested in the distance, the tragedy of the missed connection.

'Dear Renfrew,' said Ignatio, patting my hand, 'you overthink things.'

One touch of his hand and I was immediately greedy for more. Had I imagined it or was there was more to it – a kind of blue charge?

I leant across the table and kissed him quickly, boldly. His lips were oddly soft. I had never kissed a man before. The bristle on his chin was abrasive, but not harshly so. Witnessing his face was like leaning out over the guttering of a high roof. What next? Ignatio now regarded me with perfect composure. Again he patted my hand.

We saw each other almost every day. My baptism was an excuse for a big party. But most of my time was spent alone.

I had this craving to be part of something long established, yet this yearning for a simpler life, I suspected, had an intolerant purism at its core. Just because somewhere was rustic seeming, didn't mean you had gone back to nature – not at all. I had abandoned my professional life for this – this manual labour, this call to unthinking-ness; the consoling beauty of my surroundings with its verdant courtyards and fields of dusty, crenellated russets.

'Carpentry, hmm?' asked Father Ignatio, on a seemingly innocent house call. 'Filled with the Josephs, are we?'

The priest mocked me sweetly. Then, suddenly, he returned the kiss I'd given him a few weeks back.

'Come, let's go for a walk.'

We held hands in the hills. The scent of wild thyme rose in rippling waves from the baked earth. Halfway up was an abandoned car with buddleia and dry grasses growing out of it. We joked about how it could have got there. Higher up, I mistook a long thick lizard for a serpent. We watched it dart into an impossibly small orifice between the stones of an ancient crumbling wall. The smells and tastes were so particular, perhaps the more so because I was a foreigner. Perhaps the experience would mark Ignatio less for this reason. At the top of the hill we looked back at the town. He pointed out my house, which lay outside the city walls. His own was somewhere behind the grey stone fortifications. We made love on a flat rock, and slept beneath the pulsing sun. I woke first and watched him sleep, the shallow rise and fall of his chest. He opened his eyes and we kissed deeply.

But as we approached the town, he dropped my hand. So later, ignoring the mournful call to vespers, I continued with my chairs.

We didn't see each other for days. I stayed indoors, unable to make the smallest decision. I focused on the fourth chair in the set, on the crest rail. I'd had great difficulty in obtaining the 12/4 rifts of stock. The wood was jumpy, coming off the bandsaw in unexpected directions. And I tried to fool myself that the chairs were my only obsession.

But by Wednesday, I had to know.

Like a prostitute, there he was behind his window. He had to be there no matter who came along to offload their burdensome intimacies. It was his job.

Parting the red velvet curtains I stooped into the box. My knees knocked against the opposite wall of the booth. There was silence. The carpenter in me couldn't overlook the exquisite woodwork. The mind's faculty for momentary distraction, no matter the gravity of a situation, was something that never ceased to amaze and please me. Perhaps in the throes of death I'd remember that the washing hadn't been taken out of the machine, or begin considering the existential position of Kierkegaard on his final walk towards the light.

I ran my hands over the seat beneath me. Hardwood, mahogany, had to be. The latticework screen was accomplished and on my way in I'd noted, as though for the first time, the fluted crest above the box, the masterful heraldry. The sensuous contact of the wood with my palms and fingertips was perhaps of itself something to atone for; maybe all pleasures were sins.

'Bless me Father for I have sinned...'

'Say seven Hail Marys and an Our Father,' said Ignatio, irritably.

Making my way back to the house, I gazed over the town's medieval walls at the fields below. Their stunted vines, chopped back to gnarled stumps now that the harvest was over, seemed the very picture of thwarted ambition.

The owners would return on Friday. I could make a mad dash for it, spend the next forty-eight hours up a ladder. Placing the chair between my legs, I leant down and began to sand its balusters.

The Cat With No Name

Hortensia occupied her sometimes terrifying mind with innocuous pastimes like embroidery and painting by numbers, liking to follow an exact pattern to get a predictable result. Running the hotel mainly involved doing the accounts and publicity, now that she had Serge to do the breakfasts and Latifah for the rooms, so she found herself with more spare time than ever before. The time demanded to be filled, not frittered away. But even when things were easier, she had a problem with the present, preferring instead to dream of the future or dwell in, whilst mulling over, the past, so that the idea of the present could be characterised by these thoughts of an unreachable elsewhere. The present, after all, was infinitesimal, sandwiched as it was between the looming pillars of time past and time to come – blink and you missed it – yes, the present was nothing but the blink you had missed. Cats though, seemed to revel in the present, insouciant little Zen Masters. And as she looked over at her furry companion, she saw that he was readying himself to pounce. Behind the curtains, now permanently drawn, the light threw a pretty pattern, the wind through the open window causing the leaves of the coffee plant on the windowsill to dance enticingly. Cat pounced and knocked the plant off the sill, falling clumsily back onto his haunches. Embarrassed, he began busily to wash himself, spitting on his paw which he used to flatten down his ears.

'Look at you, Monsieur, pretending like nothing happened. Dignity at all costs, right? Well, of course, but who's going to clean up this mess then, my naughty pumpkin, eh?'

On her way into town one day, she stopped off in the post office to send a parcel to her friend. She scanned the notice board and saw an advert for a *gîte* for rent in les Landes. On a whim she jotted down the telephone number and, back at the hotel, phoned to arrange to go and stay there.

A week later she caught the train to Pyla-sur-Mer, changing once. She pretended to read, but thoughts of her brother intruded, images crowding their way in so that the words blurred, the spaces between them tracing fissures down the page. She read the same sentence seven times. Go back and understand this time, she told herself.

He was in a silver drawer, like lockers at the gym. They pulled him out and she identified him, turning away. That had been that. She couldn't cry, not then and not since. She was a monster, *voilà tout*.

The *gîte* was a way out of town, which the owner hadn't warned her about. She took a taxi there and the car pulled up in front of an enormous gated house with purple-painted shutters, which clashed garishly with the muted landscape. The house was painted a pale peach and its gravel gardens were laid out in a low box maze. Next to the house was a small lodge, which must be the *gîte*. It was very pretty, with dog roses clambering up around the windows. The owner came out of the big house and introduced himself, Monsieur Tourbillon. He handed her the keys and she let herself in.

Hotel owner herself, she hadn't thought to ask whether she should bring her own linen. When she went to hint to Monsieur Tourbillon about it, he shrugged non-committally, although he must have an abundance of sheets and pillowcases in his grand house. Irritated, she asked if he would please call her another taxi. When the taxi arrived she asked the driver to drop her somewhere where they sold bed linen.

She bought the sheets and pillowcases, taking ages to choose, as if it mattered, and crouched to pet a small dog tied up outside the shop. The metal blinds on some of the other shops were already going down.

She drank a coffee inside a beautiful café with large gold mirrors on its walls. The sounds of clinking cutlery and the coffee machine lulled her to a momentary peace, but almost immediately the thoughts returned. She left payment in the plastic dish and walked out onto the street. She strode towards the sea and down a little track behind the dunes.

She had seen him dead a second time. The embalmers had done too good a job. There were flowers everywhere, some plastic and some real. His skin looked waxy and pallid like the petals of the lilies in their urn-like vases, whose scent she found so overpowering. A plaster Madonna overlooked him and the kitsch finitude of the whole scene, as if he were just part of some tidy display, literally made her retch. She'd had to run outside to vomit against a wall.

Climbing the dunes, sand got in her shoes. And there was the Sea, magnificent. The light, the air.

A little boy in a red coat was flying a kite while his dad fussed around him. The sand stretched out like a desert. She sat down and scooped up cool handfuls of it, pouring it over her shins. She lay down in it and moved her arms and legs like a child making snow angels.

Between the shore and a sandbar the water was calm, but beyond this the breakers bowled in, blue over green with a dark shine like magpie feathers. The Sea's crashing cymbals worked like magic on her. She closed her eyes.

Later she found a phone booth and called Latifah.

'Hôtel des Capucines.'

'Hello, yes, it's me.'

'So, how's it going?'

'Not bad. It's so beautiful here. How's Cat?'

'He's well. Well fed. Don't worry. So what's it like? I don't know why you chose the springtime to visit the beach.'

'You know me, always everything back to front.'

'The main thing is that you get some rest.'

'That's what I'm aiming for.'

It was cold and night was falling. She caught another taxi back to the *gîte*. This was getting to be an expensive trip; she might as well have stayed in one of the fancy hotels on the Corniche. But, saying that, why book a busman's holiday? She let herself in and made up the bed with the starchy new linen. Normally, she would have put it in the wash first. Then she went downstairs and lit a fire. The potbellied wood burner was like something from a Russian fairy tale. She put the TV on and watched an episode of an American tele-series about would-be lovers on a boat. She couldn't concentrate on anything so banal and thoughts of suicide returned, his, but also potentially, hers. She would choose the easy way out, an overdose. But she didn't think she would act on it. She left the TV on for company and made herself a simple meal with the supplies she had brought. People called it a selfish act. It was selfish, but not in the way they meant. Other people just didn't figure; it had its own logic. And anyway, when you were in that state you assumed that loved ones would be better off without you, so to that extent it was a selfless act. Yes, selfless, less of the self, to the point of obliteration.

But self-obsessed? For sure. If she had called him that day, or turned up at his door, he wouldn't have done it. So to that extent others did figure, but only in the form of a diversion, an event. Maybe it would only have postponed the inevitable. Or maybe not. Every state of mind was fleeting, after all, even a years-long depression.

There was a knock at the door. It was Monsieur Tourbillon holding a bottle of wine.

'Will you have a glass with me?'

'Yes, gladly. Come in.'

He plonked himself down heavily on the little sofa. She brought two glasses and a cork screw. She knelt on the rug, not wanting the proximity of the cramped sofa, and there was nowhere else to sit.

He asked what she did in life and she told him that she was a hotel owner, like him. They talked about the business, the paradoxical loneliness when surrounded by people. At least he didn't have to do the breakfasts, she said, and he agreed, saying that he was a night owl and a late riser. He brought the conversation back to loneliness. She worried that he might be about to make a move on her but no; apparently he just wanted to talk. He admitted that he talked to himself, the first sign of madness. Well in that case I'm mad too, she said, but I don't speak in sentences, I just come out with snatches of phrases, random words, 'Idiot' being the most usual. They laughed. He asked her if she wanted to play cards and she said she would and why not for money? He rummaged in the corner cupboard amongst all the board games and found a deck. He dealt quickly and they played a game of Koi-Koi. Hortensia won and they played again. She won three times in a row. Monsieur Tourbillon, or Paul, as he insisted that she call him, laughed a little tensely and said that he'd better call it a night.

In the morning she got up and made coffee in a jug. She'd bought croissants in Casino the day before and they were a bit dry, so she warmed them in the oven. She took her breakfast out onto the patio. There was a high brick wall obscured by honeysuckle gone crazy, in which a pair of goldfinches were singing. She went back in and washed the plate and cup. Paul's face appeared at the window, startling her. She let him in. He gave her 270 Francs in change, her winnings from the night before, and said it had been a pleasure to meet her. He offered to drive her to the station and she accepted. When he left to get the car out of the garage she stripped the bed and stuffed the linen into her bag. Paul pulled up in front of the *gîte* as she closed the door behind her. She threw her bag into the backseat and handed him the house keys.

On the way to the station he told her about his first marriage.

'She was a real bitch,' he said.

There wasn't much to answer to that so after an awkward pause he changed the subject.

He offered to carry her bag onto the platform but she said that she'd manage. He asked for her phone number. She began to reel it off but, changing her mind, gave a false digit at the end. The train came. She got on and found a quiet carriage. Suddenly ravenous, she ate a whole bar of chocolate. She read magazines on the first train and dozed on the second.

Back at the hotel, she and Latifah shared a snacky meal together and Hortensia told Latifah about Monsieur Tourbillon, the sheets, and the card game. Latifah told her about a particularly annoying guest who had stained the sheets and left a 30 centimes tip.

That night Hortensia let the cat sleep on her bed. He stretched luxuriantly, rolled onto his back and let her pat his plush belly before curling up with his head propped on primly crossed paws. She, on the other hand, didn't sleep at all. Eventually she got up and went into the kitchenette. Her apartment consisted of three rooms: this one, the bedroom and a tiny bathroom. She took a packet of cigarettes down from the cupboard; she'd started again since Gilles died.

She sat smoking at the table. The cigarettes were sexy, colourful ones, but too short. She smoked two in a row, one pinky magenta, the next one mustard yellow.

Her mind was punishing her. She recalled the time her icecream had fallen on the sand and she had pushed him over so he'd lose his too. She remembered pinching his records and deliberately scratching them. Telling him he was adopted but not to tell Maman that he knew in case he upset her. The memories kept coming; the forlorn look on his face – it was a kind of torture. If she had only looked after him better, been the big sister she should have been, none of this would have happened. She lit a pistachio green cigarette. The kitchen stank of smoke. Cat jumped up onto the table and came to her, nuzzling her cheekbone, swivelling round and putting his backside in her face, tail up, the puckered little aureole making her laugh and push him away. She fussed him as he climbed onto her lap, purring and clawing the fabric of her dressing gown.

She needed to do something mindless. She brought in the receipts box from the bedroom and stapled last month's receipts to pieces of paper, which she arranged in date order. Then she scrubbed the toilet, cleaned the sink and sprayed window-cleaner onto the mirror, buffing it up with a dry cloth. She took the broom out onto the hotel landing and began, quietly, to sweep. She boiled water for the bucket and started vigorously mopping the floor. A door opened and a bewildered looking guest peered round it.

'What are you doing?'

'I'm mopping the floor.'

'Can't you do it in the morning?'

'Yes, sorry. I hope I didn't disturb you.'

'Well you obviously did, but never mind.'

'Go on back to bed. Good night,' she said, a little too definitely. Had she been rude? She took the mop and bucket into the kitchen, swilled water down the sink and chucked some bleach in with it. Then she put the mop and bucket back in the hall cupboard, making a racket as she did so. She returned to the kitchen and smoked some more. Dawn came, and with it, the sound of birdsong, filling her heart with doom.

She showered, dressed, and went down to the main kitchen where Serge was lighting the oven.

'Morning,' he said. 'You're up early.'

'I couldn't sleep,' she said, helping herself to coffee. Cat came in and wove a figure of eight around her ankles.

'Puss,' she said, 'you little opportunist. Now, you'll be wanting some of this good fish, won't you? Certain individuals won't eat their greens, hmm?'

She took a mackerel filet from the fridge and peeled off its slimy skin, breaking the flesh into chunks, which she put into Cat's cut glass dish.

'I'm going for a walk Serge. When he's eaten that, can you let him out?'

'No problem.'

She walked along by the river; the same old walk. Monsieur Cotillard was fishing near the bridge.

'Hello Madame.'

'Hi.'

A little further on a group of ducks were involved in some kind of fracas. Hortensia stopped to watch. A group of mallard drakes had gathered round a female and were pecking her. Their quacks rose and fell in jabbering clicks. One of them mounted her, pressing her right down, and another one climbed onto her head. They were gang-raping her! Hortensia grabbed a stone and threw it at them. The ducks dispersed, then re-formed, quibbling all the louder. She scrabbled about for more stones and threw a volley of them, one hitting the drake who was crushing the female duck, right on his emerald dog-collar. The ducks dispersed, some waddling quickly into the shrubbery, others to the river. You had to meddle with cruel nature whenever you got the chance to.

At the funeral she'd worn dark glasses, feeling like a hypocrite. They must have thought she was wearing them to hide her tears, whereas she was really trying to hide the lack of any. Everyone had something nice to say. Exhausting. She felt cored out, a spinning vortex moving up through her insides, a tornado with nowhere to go. There was a memorial planned for the summer. If she could write poems, she'd write one for him and read it out. He was the poet though. She had the sudden impression of his hands, long, languid fingers, the way they touched the piano keys. She wished she could lean over and kiss the crown of his head, tell him it would be all right, he just had to stick around.

An upturned boat partially blocked the path. The grasses were high already and soon she came to the edge of the woods. Through the gaps in the trees were patches of smoky violet where the bluebells grew. Memory was exhaustive; he could be kept close through all the mind's thousands of film clips. The trick was not to keep replaying the same ones too often, or they became meaningless. Real photos helped to fill the gaps creating both false and true recollections – who could say which? – of a particular day, and in this way you could stay ever-present in the vast realm of the past, reviving tracts of spent time in the act of archiving them, all whilst maintaining the fiction of a continuum, of progress. You should record everything, even if the means of doing so were never exactly right. She turned back.

That afternoon she wrote letters and took care of business. The doorbell rang. One of the guests? An inexplicable sense of dread descended upon her. She opened the door and there stood Jean-Yves Bertrand, holding a box.

'He just ran out,' said Jean-Yves, 'I braked but it was too late. I'm so sorry.'

Hortensia looked at the box. She looked at Jean-Yves and then back at the box.

'Thank you… It wasn't your fault.'

She accepted his dreadful gift and closed the door. Had she just spoken? Her words echoed unnaturally in her imagination, as though voiced by someone else. She stared uncomprehending at the box in her hands. The box was an object. Cat was dead, so he, too, must be an object. His paw was outstretched, an offering. His hand in hers, they are standing at the brown margin where Land meets Sea, and waves are hissing in, fast and low, near the shore with glassy clarity, further out, in intesities of teal and jade. 'Come on, race you in!'

The box judders in her outstretched hands, so heavy.

She holds it carefully going up the stairs and, once in the kitchen, sets it down on the table with a sigh of grief, of utter exhaustion. He could be sleeping. Bedtime stories – she used to do all the voices. His fur takes on a reddish tint in the brazen sunlight even the curtains can't keep out; tiny kinks, as though it has been crimped. Nights shared, the dull weight of him on her legs. And now this, the ragged, senseless end of the world with no fanfare. She leans into the box and puts her face next to his. The dumb serenity of beasts, his perpetual half-smile. The truth was, he should not have loved her, she didn't deserve it, and so his love was a gift outside of the economy of exchange. Yes, she looked after him, but his love moved beyond the cupboard and into the core of her; it was impalpable, a swirling movement signalled in his richly sonorous purr. She might be unlovable but he loved her all the same. He was her everything. She would have to use the past tense now. And to whom? Their love was a kind of complicity, like an illicit liaison, unwitnessed and unsanctioned beyond the dear immediacy of their bond.

She used to wipe the food from around his mouth and walk him to school when Maman was having a bad day. He would hold her hand to cross the road and to balance on the high wall. She beat up his bullies for him and carried on tying his shoelaces even when he knew how. Beasts, why must they always signal something else? Metaphorical beings, furry little stand-ins; dependent, unquestioning, unthreatening. A child on the other hand: all of the above, bar the fur and the questions. Questions, questions. Why? Why then and why now? His squishy belly – the way he would invite her to rub it, then pounce on her hand, catching it in his slack jaw and kicking with his rabbit-like feet. A life in miniature – the blood and gore, feathers and entrails, shit and piss, grazed knees, tears and sticking plasters, hairballs puked up and kisses, reparations, the terrible loneliness of the carer. Politeness, the carapace of existence, quelling the savagery of the heart. And with each death, blame. She should not have gone out! She should have been there as much in an emotional sense as in a physical one, prevention and cure. He was always rubbish at knots, butter-fingered little fuckwit, and now this.

The last phone call, another request for money and she'd more or less told him to get lost. That dolt Serge should never have let him out the front. Well she would go right ahead and fire him! No, she probably wouldn't, but still. She ran her fingers through her hair then reached into the box and slid her hands under his flank and shoulder. He was still warm. Cradling him like an infant, she felt drunk, woozy. There was no blood, she checked all over, no sign of injury. His eyes were closed, inky little flicks. She willed him to life with all her might, screwing her eyes tight, holding her breath, whilst gently squeezing his paw with its dry liquorice pads. But nothing, no miracle ensued.

He had been with her for a lifetime; well, for his lifetime anyway, ever since he was a kitten – those coltish legs, the round stare, his hammy surprises – a span of only fourteen years, but during which time they had rarely been apart. A dozen terms of endearment, but he never had a proper name, never needed one. He was simply Cat, and all that a cat could be. She put her face close to his, kissed his blunt forehead, tickling the soft pelt behind his ears. Her heart must break, surely. She was a foolish old woman, granted. But really, what was the point in any of it? Well, she supposed, it would all be over soon enough. She sat down, lit a Sobranie, and let herself cry.

END

POLLY TUCKETT speaks with a fresh, contemporary voice steeped in the literary traditions of Flaubert, Maupassant and Proust. She is a Leicester-based writer of short fiction and poetry and her work has appeared in many print and online journals, including *Areté* and *Brittle Star*. Her stories have been shortlisted for the Bridport and Fish prizes. She is currently working on a cycle of character-themed poems in French.

If you've enjoyed this book, help us get the word out about our Thumbprint chapbooks by sharing your thoughts on social media or over a lovely cuppa with friends, or by writing a review on our website or wherever you bought your copy. Thank you so much from all of us here at Stonewood Press.

---

www.stonewoodpress.co.uk

Other Stonewood Press Thumbprints:

Philip Levine's Good Ear by Lisa Kelly

When You Lived Inside the Walls and Other Stories by Krishan Coupland

A Massacre of Hummingbirds by Paul Blake

Green City by Sue MacIntyre

Dad's slideshow by Di Slaney

Hoad and Other Stories by Sarah Passingham

Earthworks by Jacqueline Gabbitas

www.stonewoodpress.co.uk

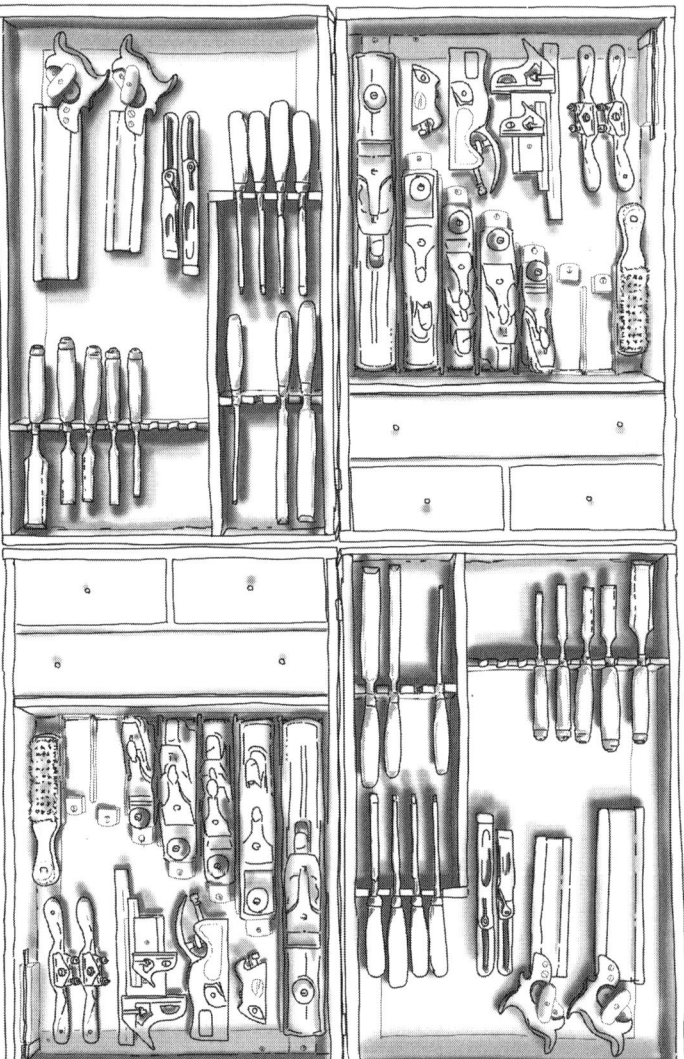

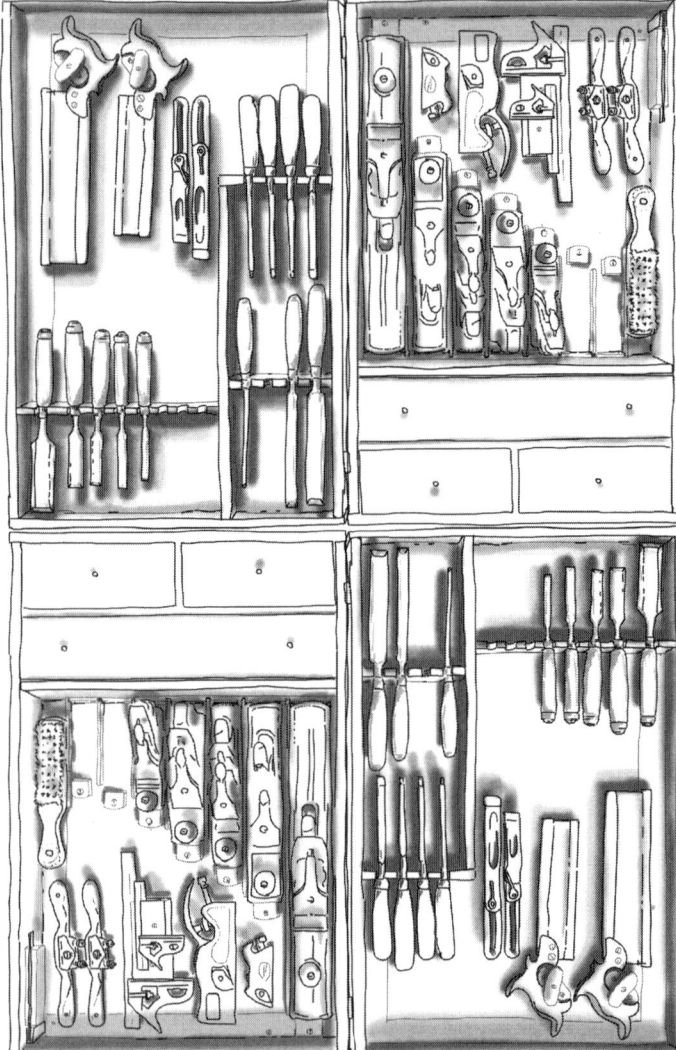